W9-BUJ-724

MAIN

Young Arthur

Young Arthur

by Robert D. San Souci
illustrated by Jamichael Henterly

A Doubleday Book for Young Readers

Long ago, as King Uther and Merlin watched, a fiery dragon-shape blazed among the stars over Stonehenge, foretelling the birth of Arthur, the greatest king of all . . .

King Uther heard the baby's wail and leaped to his feet. There was a sharp rap at the chamber door, and a servant entered grinning happily. "You have a son," he told the king. Uther's joy knew no bounds. When he was ushered into Queen Igerna's bedchamber, Uther looked lovingly at mother and son. "The boy's name shall be Arthur," he declared, "and he shall be a great king. For Merlin has foretold that he will one day rule the greatest kingdom under heaven."

But Uther's happiness did not last. His beloved queen died soon after Arthur's birth, and sadness sapped the king's spirit. He lost interest in ruling, and Merlin was unable to rouse him from his melancholy. "Unrest grows throughout the land," Merlin warned. "Your old foes are rising in rebellion. Give the babe into my keeping, for you have enemies even at court."

Anxious for his son's safety, Uther agreed. So Merlin, disguised as a beggar, took the infant Arthur to Sir Ector and his lady, who lived some distance from the court and all its dangers. He told them nothing about the child, save that his name was Arthur. The couple had recently lost their infant son and welcomed Arthur as their own.

Soon rebellion divided the kingdom. Uther, reclaiming his old spirit, rallied his knights and barons. With Merlin always beside him, he drove back his enemies.

But as Uther celebrated his victory in the town of Verulum, traitors poisoned the town's wells. The king and his loyal followers were stricken. Merlin alone escaped. Though he tried his healing arts on Uther, he was forced to confess, "Sire, there is no remedy."

"Then," said the dying monarch, "I declare that my son shall be king of all this realm after me. God's blessing and mine be upon him." With these words, Uther died.

When the rebels entered Verulum, only Merlin was alive.

"Tell us where Uther's son is hidden," they demanded, "so that we can slay him and end Uther's line."

But Merlin vanished before their eyes.

Young Arthur was raised as a son in Sir Ector's house. He learned to read and write alongside his foster brother, Kay, who was four years older. By the time he was fifteen, Arthur was a tall, handsome, quick-witted lad. Though he had great strength, he also had a gentle manner.

Kay, who had recently been knighted, decided to train Arthur in the knightly arts himself. But Kay was vain and jealous of the favor Arthur found with their father, so he was a harsh taskmaster. Arthur came away from his lessons in swordsmanship with many bruises and cuts. When he complained, Kay replied, "A knight must be thick-skinned and ready to bear even grievous wounds without flinching." Yet if Arthur so much as pricked his brother, Kay would bellow loudly for the physician.

Eventually Kay appointed Arthur his apprentice. This was an honor the younger boy would happily have forgone. However, seeing that Sir Ector wished it so, Arthur sighed and agreed. But he felt in his heart that he already was a knight, though no lord had dubbed him such.

Both Arthur and Kay knew it was vital to learn the arts of war. The kingdom was still at the mercy of upstart lords who ruled by fire and sword.

The story of Uther's lost son, the true heir to the throne, would have been forgotten but for Merlin. One Christmas Eve, the long-absent magician reappeared and summoned the bishops, lords, and common folk to London's square. There he drove a broadsword halfway into a huge stone. Written on the blade in blazing gold letters were the words: "Whoso pulleth out the sword from this stone is born the rightful King of England."

In the days that followed, knights and barons, cowherds and bakers, an endless parade of would-be kings eagerly pulled at the sword. But none could loosen it, let alone draw it forth.

When they accused Merlin of trickery, he said, "The rightful king has not yet come. God will make him known at the proper time."

Now it happened that a great tournament was held in London. Among those who came were Sir Ector, Sir Kay, and young Arthur, who served Kay. So eager was the boy to see the jousts that he forgot to pack Kay's sword. There was great upset when the mistake was discovered.

"Woe to you, boy," snarled Kay, "if your error costs me the victory I would otherwise win today!"

Even Sir Ector scolded Arthur and ordered, "Go back directly and fetch the missing sword."

Angry at his carelessness and impatient to see the contests, Arthur started homeward. Then he suddenly reined in his horse.

In the deserted city square was a massive stone with a sword plunged into its center. "Surely that sword is as good as the one left at home," he said. "I will borrow it. When Kay is finished, I will return it to this curious monument."

So saying, he dismounted, scrambled up the stone, took the sword handle, and tugged. The sword did not move. Impatient to return to the tournament, he pulled again. This time, the sword slid easily out of the stone. In his haste, he did not notice the words upon the blade. Shoving the weapon into his belt, he remounted and raced to where Sir Kay waited his turn upon the field.

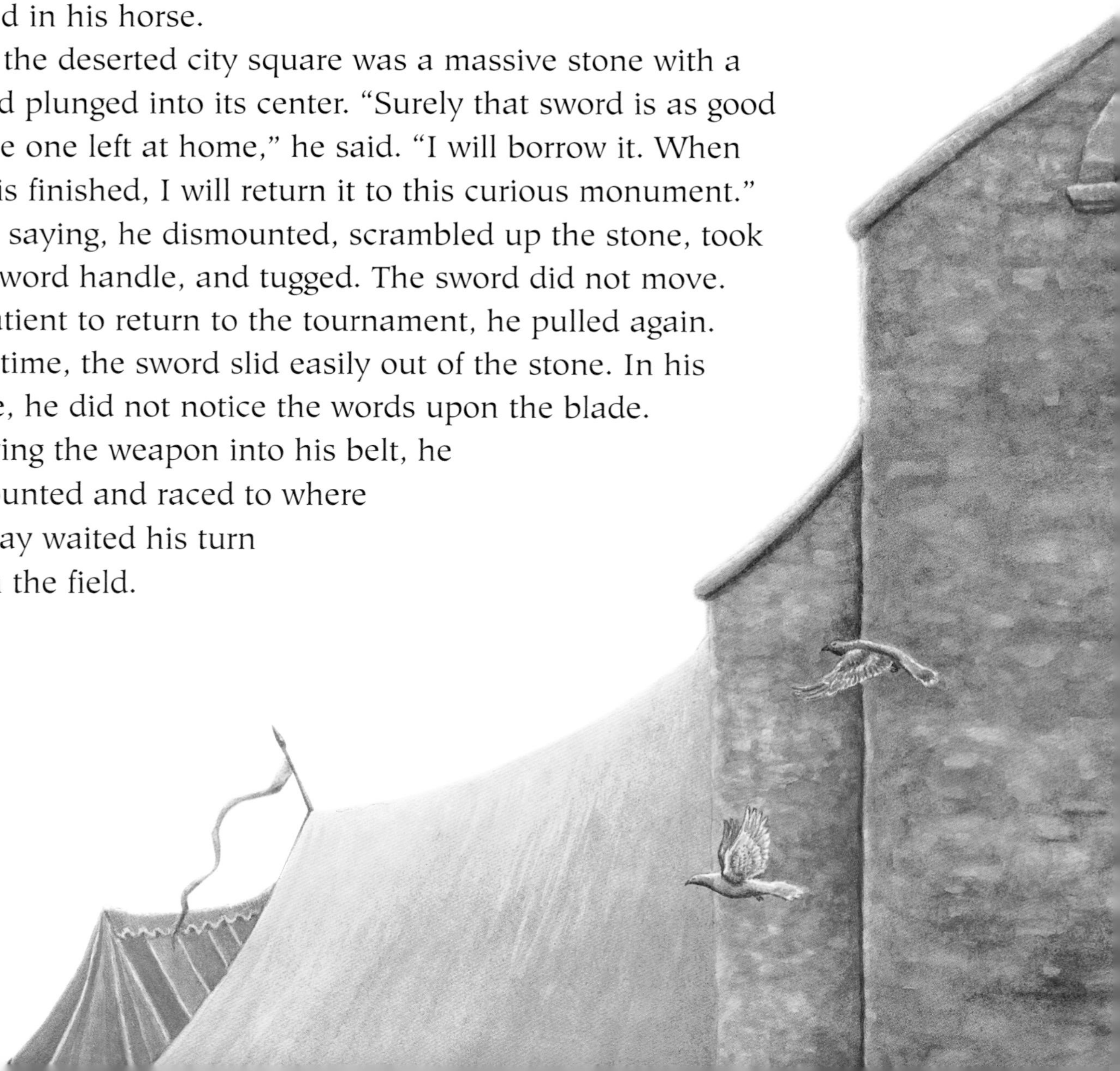

The moment he saw the golden words upon the blade, Kay began to tremble with excitement. When Arthur asked what was amiss, Kay shouted, "Go! Get away! You have caused enough trouble."

But Arthur was curious. So he followed as Kay ran to Sir Ector. "Look, Father!" cried Kay. "Here is the sword of the stone. Therefore, it is I who must be king of all this land!"

When Sir Ector and the others saw the sword and read the golden inscription, they began to shout, "The sword from the stone! The king's sword!"

Hearing only this much, Arthur thought that he had stolen a king's weapon. As people hurried excitedly toward Kay, Arthur spurred his horse away, certain he had committed a great crime.

Looking back, he saw Kay and Sir Ector ride off, surrounded by the greatest lords of the realm. Were they taking Kay to trial? he wondered. Had he brought ruin upon Sir Ector's household?

"A true knight would not run away," he said to himself, "and I am a true knight in my heart." Fearful, but determined to do what was right, the boy wheeled his horse around.

The great square was now filled with people. Just how terrible a crime had he committed?

Upon the stone stood Kay, holding the sword. The crowd shouted each time he held the blade aloft. Then silence fell over the throng: Merlin had appeared at the edge of the square. People stood aside to let the magician approach the stone.

"Are you the one who pulled the sword from the stone?" Merlin asked.

"I am holding it, am I not?" Kay replied.

"The rightful king could pull it free a hundred times," said Merlin. "Slip the sword into the groove and pull it out again."

With a shrug, Kay reinserted the sword. But when he tried to jerk it free, it would not budge.

Suddenly all eyes turned toward Arthur, who was pushing his way through the crowd, bellowing at the top of his lungs. "It wasn't Kay's fault! I brought him the sword!"

Merlin peered closely at Arthur. Then he smiled and said, "Climb up and draw the sword from the stone."

Uncertainly Arthur clambered up beside Kay. Grasping the pommel, he easily pulled the sword out.

Then Merlin cried, "This is Arthur, son of Uther Pendragon, Britain's destined king."

An astonished Sir Ector knelt to pay the boy homage, followed by Kay and many others. But all around, there was growing confusion and dispute. Some cried, "It is the will of heaven! Long live the king!" while others cried, "It is Merlin's plot to put a beardless boy, a puppet, on the throne, and so rule the land."

The cries of "Long live King Arthur!" soon carried the day. But many powerful knights and barons rode away angry, vowing never to accept Arthur as their king.

Arthur was crowned in London. But it was the custom for Britain's high king to be crowned a second time as King of Wales. So Arthur, Merlin, and his court rode to the old walled city of Caerleon.

On the day of his coronation feast, enemy lords laid siege to the city. They breached the gates and battled their way into the great hall.

Just when all seemed lost, Arthur rose up like a blazing fire against his enemies. In the struggle, his sword was shattered. Brandishing his broken weapon, he led a counterattack that drove the rebels from the hall and from the city.

Though the city was secure, the king's forces were outnumbered by the enemy beyond the walls. More rebels joined the siege of Caerleon hourly.

In the great hall, Arthur stared unhappily at his broken sword. "If I had a proper king's sword, I would rout those rebels once and for all," he boasted.

"You have courage and a strong right arm," said Merlin. "In a short time, you have shown you have the makings of a just and wise ruler. These things are more important than a sword, no matter how finely made. The people trust you."

"Yes," Arthur said with a thin smile, "but I would more easily trust myself if I had a proper sword."

"Then you shall have it!" said Merlin. "Come, we have a great distance to travel in a short time."

"How can we go anywhere?" Arthur protested. "We are surrounded by enemies."

"Take my hand," said Merlin. "Don't be afraid. If you speak or cry out, you will undo everything."

Without hesitation, Arthur clasped Merlin's hand. It seemed to him that they were wrapped in pale smoke. Then they flew like ghosts along corridors, unseen by the guards. They passed through the huge doors of the hall, though they were closed. Down the deserted streets they raced.

Arthur felt excited, afraid, dizzy. Many times he choked back a cry. But he kept silent, his fingers twined with Merlin's.

They reached the city walls, and poured like rising smoke up the battlements; they poured down the outer walls like rainwater. They sped past the tents and watchfires of the enemy camp, then across the meadows and through the trees beyond.

The two stopped suddenly beside a broad, misty lake. Nearby, a little boat rocked gently at the water's edge.

"Get in," said Merlin.

Arthur did so, and the magician followed.

"There are no oars," said Arthur.

"They are not needed," Merlin replied. Indeed, the boat was already drifting toward the center of the lake, where the reflected moon shimmered like a pool of liquid silver. When they reached the brightness, a woman's arm thrust up, holding a great sword.

"This is the sword you seek—one truly worthy of a king. It is called Excalibur," said Merlin. "Take it."

Arthur took hold of the handle by wrapping his fingers around the woman's pale fingers. At his touch, the ghostly arm vanished, and the sword remained in his grasp.

Then the boat carried them swiftly back to shore. There they were wrapped again in Merlin's smoky magic, and returned unseen to the great hall.

When he found himself seated once more before the great fire, Arthur wondered if he had had a waking dream. But Excalibur lay across his knees.

At dawn, Arthur, brandishing Excalibur, led his army against the enemy just emerging from their tents. They had assumed that Arthur would keep his weaker force behind the walls. While the rebels hastened to form battle lines, Merlin magically scattered their watchfires. The flame and smoke from burning tents added to their confusion.

But it was Arthur who carried the day. The marvelous sword he carried flashed in the light of the rising sun as it rose and fell, rose and fell. Excalibur seemed to have a life of its own as it flickered right or left to wound or slay an enemy.

The battle was fierce, and where the fighting was the most desperate, there was King Arthur, raging like a young lion. When the three most powerful rebel lords set upon him, Excalibur burned as bright as the sun itself, blinding Arthur's enemies. Then he fell upon them and drove them off. And when the knights saw their lords in flight, they broke and ran.

Then the common folk of Caerleon rushed out, armed with clubs and staves. They harried the stragglers until none of the enemy remained upon the field.

King Arthur had won his first battle. Though his soldiers urged him to pursue and punish his foes, he said, "We need fear those lords no longer. They are beaten and have nothing left them but their honor. I will not slay them to take that away."

Merlin nodded, saying, "Such mercy may well turn those enemies to friends in time."

"Friends or enemies, I will meet them as true king of the realm," Arthur replied, sheathing Excalibur.

"Now," said Merlin, "your real work begins. You must raise the castle my dreams name Camelot, and gather around you the greatest knights from near and far. Then you will establish a reign of such nobility, justice, and wisdom that all ages will celebrate Arthur the King, whose fame will grow with every passing generation."

For Karen Wojtyla . . .
Warmest wishes without end,
To a five–star editor,
Who's a multi–star friend!
—R.S.S.

For Lael Lupine
and Skye Juniper
—J.H.

Author's Note

For this retelling I consulted such traditional sources as *History of the Kings of Britain* by Geoffrey of Monmouth; *Arthurian Romances* by Chrétien de Troyes; *Idylls of the King* by Alfred, Lord Tennyson; *King Arthur: Tales of the Round Table,* edited by Andrew Lang; and *The Story of King Arthur and His Knights* by Howard Pyle. Other helpful volumes include *King Arthur* by Norma Lorre Goodrich; *The Quest for Arthur's Britain,* edited by Geoffrey Ashe; *The Arthurian Encyclopedia,* edited by Norris J. Lacy; and *An Arthurian Reader: Selections from Arthurian Legend, Scholarship and Story,* edited by John Matthews.

A Doubleday Book for Young Readers
Published by Bantam Doubleday Dell Publishing Group, Inc.
1540 Broadway, New York, New York 10036

Doubleday and the portrayal of an anchor with a dolphin are trademarks of
Bantam Doubleday Dell Publishing Group, Inc.

Library of Congress Cataloging-in-Publication Data

San Souci, Robert D.
Young Arthur / by Robert D. San Souci ; illustrated by Jamichael Henterly.
p. cm.
Summary: Recounts the story of King Arthur's boyhood, the sword in the stone, his first victorious battle, and his unification of a new kingdom.
ISBN 0-385-32268-2 (alk. paper)
1. Arthurian romances—Adaptations. [1. Arthur, King—Legends. 2. Knights and knighthood—Folklore. 3. Folklore—England.] I. Henterly, Jamichael, ill. II. Title.
PZ8.1.S227Yj 1997
[398.2]—dc20
[E] 96-27248
CIP
AC

The text of this book is set in 14-point Hiroshige.
Book design by Kimberly M. Adlerman
Manufactured in the United States of America
November 1997
10 9 8 7 6 5 4 3 2 1